# SMALL GAME HUNTING

ABBY BADACH DOYLE

Gareth Stevens
PUBLISHING

Please visit our website, www.garethstevens.com. For a free color catalog of all our high-quality books, call toll free 1-800-542-2595 or fax 1-877-542-2596.

**Cataloging-in-Publication Data**
Names: Doyle, Abby Badach.
Title: Small game hunting / Abby Badach Doyle.
Description: New York : Gareth Stevens Publishing, 2023. | Series: Totally into fishing and hunting | Includes glossary and index.
Identifiers: ISBN 9781538280119 (pbk.) | ISBN 9781538280133 (library bound) | ISBN 9781538280126 (6pack) | ISBN 9781538280140 (ebook)
Subjects: LCSH: Small game hunting–Juvenile literature.
Classification: LCC SK340.D69 2023 | DDC 799.2'5–dc23

Portions of this work were originally authored by Kaylee Gilmore and published as *We're Going Small Game Hunting*. All new material in this edition is authored by Abby Badach Doyle.

Published in 2023 by
**Gareth Stevens Publishing**
29 East 21st Street
New York, NY 10010

Copyright © 2023 Gareth Stevens Publishing

Editor: Abby Badach Doyle
Designer: Michael Flynn

Photo credits: Cover, pp. 1 moosehenderson/Shutterstock.com; series background (camo) Alexvectors/Shutterstock.com; p. 4 Renamarie/Shutterstock.com; p. 5 Edwin Godinho/Shutterstock.com; p. 7 YevgeniyDr/Shutterstock.com; p. 8 K Steve Cope/Shutterstock.com; p. 9 William Booth/Shutterstock.com; p. 10 Andrew Park/Shutterstock.com; p. 11 Tom Reichner/Shutterstock.com; p. 13 Stephen Brashear/AP Photo; p. 14 Ken Weinrich/Shutterstock.com; p. 15 mmpixel91/Shutterstock.com; p. 17 ZoranOrcik/Shutterstock.com; p. 18 Mary Swift/Shutterstock.com; p. 19 Vitalii_Mamchuk/Shutterstock.com; p. 21 Manamana/Shutterstock.com; p. 23 Holly Kuchera/Shutterstock.com; p. 24 MelaniWright/Shutterstock.com; p. 25 Geza Farkas/Shutterstock.com; p. 26 Rabbitti/Shutterstock.com; p. 27 Digital_Clipart/Shutterstock.com; p. 27 (coyote footprints, fox footprints, frame) Digital_Clipart/Shutterstock.com; p. 27 (squirrel footprints) vectortatu/Shutterstock.com; p. 27 (rabbit footprints, raccoon footprints) WinWin artlab/Shutterstock.com; p. 27 (groundhog footprints) OnD/Shutterstock.com; p. 28 Jim Cumming/Shutterstock.com; p. 29 Roman Kosolapov/Shutterstock.com.

Printed in the United States of America

**A NOTE TO READERS**
Always talk with a parent or teacher before proceeding with any of the activities found in this book. Some activities require adult supervision.

**A NOTE TO PARENTS AND TEACHERS**
This book was written to be informative and entertaining. Some of the activities in this book require adult supervision. Please talk with your child or student before allowing them to proceed with any hunting activities. The author and publisher specifically disclaim any liability for injury or damages that may result from use of information in this book.

Some of the images in this book illustrate individuals who are models. The depictions do not imply actual situations or events.

CPSIA compliance information: Batch #CSGS23: For further information contact Gareth Stevens, New York, New York at 1-800-542-2595.

Find us on

# CONTENTS

**WORDS IN THE GLOSSARY APPEAR IN BOLD TYPE THE FIRST TIME THEY ARE USED IN THE TEXT.**

# LET'S HUNT!

You've likely seen small game animals like squirrels, rabbits, or groundhogs around your neighborhood. However, hunting them is a totally different adventure. If you are a new hunter, small game hunting is a great way to get started.

Some people hunt small game to practice hunting larger animals. Other people like the **challenge** of small game hunting all on its own. Many small animals are good at hiding. Also, the smaller the animal . . . the smaller the **target**!

GRAY SQUIRREL

Squirrels are one of the most common small game animals.

5

# SMALL GAME ANIMALS

"Small game" refers to small, wild animals that are hunted for sport or meat. These animals usually weigh less than 40 pounds (18.1 kg). Each state has laws about small game animals, such as which ones you are and aren't allowed to hunt.

This book mostly talks about **mammals**. Small game mammals include rabbits, squirrels, foxes, groundhogs, and coyotes. Game birds such as ducks, geese, pheasants, and grouse are also considered small game in some states.

## KNOW THE FACTS!

In certain states, you can hunt frogs, snakes, or turtles. Porcupines and armadillos are also considered small game in some places if you have a hunting **license**. Porcupines don't have much meat, but some people say they're tasty!

Groundhogs are also called woodchucks,
whistle-pigs, or marmots.

7

# IN SEASON

The time period you are allowed to hunt a certain kind of animal is known as its "season." In some states, certain small game animals are always in season. Others can only be hunted for a few months of the year.

An animal's season is usually when the population is at its highest.

Imagine you're hunting squirrels, and you have a perfect shot at a rabbit. Don't shoot unless you're sure rabbits are in season. Each state has its own laws for hunting seasons. Make sure you know your state's laws before you go hunting.

## KNOW THE FACTS!

It is against the law to hunt animals that aren't in season. When people break the law to hunt, it is known as poaching.

# WHERE TO GO HUNTING

Small game animals live in many **habitats**, from forests to fields. Small animals, such as rabbits and squirrels, like to hide in brush piles. These provide cover from weather or predators.

## KNOW THE FACTS!

If you can, visit an area before hunting there. Walk around and keep an eye out for signs of small game, such as animal trails and droppings.

RABBIT DROPPINGS

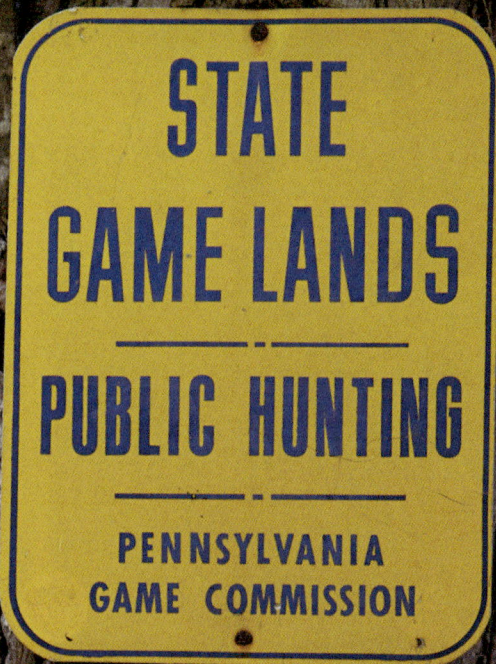

Your state's wildlife department website will list state game lands near you.

Many hunters hunt in special areas called state game lands that are owned by the government. These are lands that are set aside for hunters to use. However, hikers and dog walkers can use these areas too. Don't take a shot unless you're sure no other people or pets are around.

# KNOW THE RULES

Before going hunting, you'll need to take a safety course. Once you pass the test, you'll be able to purchase a hunting license from your state. Depending on your age and where you live, you may need a licensed adult to hunt with you.

Most states allow you to shoot several small game animals in a single day. The "bag limit" is the top number of animals you're allowed to kill. Hunters who go over this number are breaking the law.

## KNOW THE FACTS!

Bag limits help keep habitats and animal populations healthy.

In a safety course, you'll learn about your **weapon** and how to shoot safely. You will also learn hunting laws and first aid.

# HUNTING WITH GUNS

Shotguns are a popular choice of firearm, or gun, to hunt small game. These guns scatter many pellets, called shot, over a short range. This means you must get closer to your target, but you have a much better chance of hitting it.

## KNOW THE FACTS!

Ammunition is the name for bullets, shells, and other things fired by weapons. Choose ammunition without lead. Lead is a metal that can make animals and people sick if eaten.

SHOTGUN SHELLS

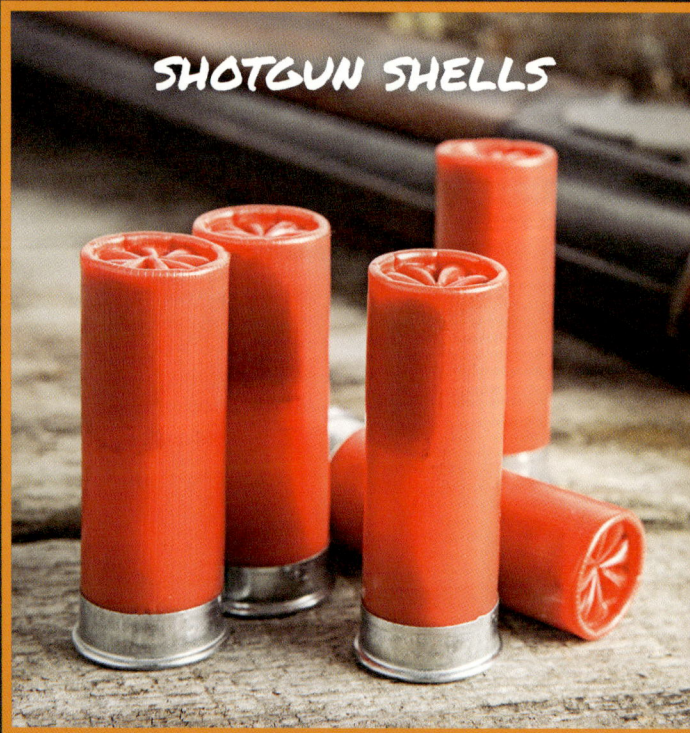

Most states require hunters to wear bright orange so other hunters can see them.

A rifle is a long gun that's held against the shoulder when fired. Rifles shoot single bullets that travel long distances, or lengths, and cause great harm. It can be harder to use a rifle to shoot a small, fast animal.

# HUNTING WITH BOWS

For a greater challenge, you can try bowhunting. This is also called archery. It is very hard to hit a small animal with an arrow. Arrows are slower than shot or bullets. The animal has more time to move after the arrow is let go.

Some hunters use a **compound** bow. This type of bow uses cables and **pulleys** that make it easier to pull back an arrow. Successful small game bowhunters have great aim . . . and practice a lot!

## KNOW THE FACTS!

Compound bows can shoot at faster speeds than **traditional** bows. However, traditional bows can be easier to load. They are also lighter to carry.

Archery is one of the oldest forms of hunting.

# HUNTING WITH DOGS

After you shoot a small game animal, its body can be hard to find in tall grass or brush. Some hunters use dogs to help. A good hunting dog has a powerful sense of smell, natural ability, and isn't scared of gunshots.

## KNOW THE FACTS!

President George Washington had dozens of hunting dogs. In fact, he helped create the **breed** of dog now known as the American foxhound.

AMERICAN FOXHOUND

The pointer breed got its name because these dogs "point" when they see an animal.

Certain breeds of dogs are easily trained to be excellent hunters. All types of hounds, such as coonhounds and bloodhounds, make great hunting helpers. Beagles are very good rabbit hunters. Retrievers are used to hunt game birds and waterfowl.

# SNEAKY SQUIRRELS

Like many other animals, squirrels are good at seeing movement. Squirrel hunters often use a method called still hunting. Still hunters move slowly and silently. They stop often to look and listen.

Squirrels usually hide in trees. If a hunter walks around the tree, the squirrel will move to the opposite side. If you're hunting in a group, one hunter can stand absolutely still while another hunter walks around the tree. The squirrel will circle until the first hunter has a shot.

## KNOW THE FACTS!

Squirrels can be hard to spot. The colors and patterns in their fur help them blend in with their surroundings. This is called camouflage.

Squirrels eat oak tree acorns and hickory tree nuts.
If you spot these, there may be squirrels nearby.

# CRAFTY RACCOONS

Raccoons are nocturnal, which means they are most active at night. For that reason, you'll have better luck hunting them in the dark. Raccoon hunting is easier with the help of dogs, such as coonhounds. Hounds can smell raccoons and corner them in trees.

Trapping an animal in a tree is called treeing. Treeing is where the phrase "barking up the wrong tree" comes from. If a hound is barking up the wrong tree, it's not a very good hunting dog!

## KNOW THE FACTS!

Raccoons are known as furbearers. These are animals that are hunted for their soft, thick fur. Foxes, mink, and beavers are furbearers too.

You can use a light or headlamp to help you spot raccoons at night.

# RUNNING RABBITS

Rabbits like to hide in heavy brush. You have to get them to show themselves before you can successfully hunt them. One method for hunting rabbits is to startle, or scare, them out of their hiding places. You can do this by walking and making noise through their habitat. Then, stop and be silent while they run into the open.

When startled, rabbits run away in a zigzag pattern.
That's when you can take your shot!

There are several kinds of cottontail rabbits found across the United States. Hares are **related** to rabbits. Hares are bigger with larger ears.

## KNOW THE FACTS!

To many hunters, one of the most satisfying parts of hunting is cooking the meat. Rabbit meat is tasty when fried, stuffed, grilled, or cooked in a stew.

Some hunters hunt just for fun. Others hunt because small game animals cause trouble on their property. Rabbits and groundhogs can destroy crops, gardens, and fields. Foxes and coyotes eat chickens. Hunting is a useful way to get rid of these pests.

These animals are usually only considered pests because there are too many of them. They might have fewer natural predators, such as wolves and bobcats, in the wild. Without predators, small game populations can grow out of control.

## KNOW THE FACTS!

Small game animals that cause trouble are also called vermin or varmints.

# SMALL GAME TRACKS

**COYOTE**

**FOX**

**GROUNDHOG**

**RABBIT**

**RACCOON**

**SQUIRREL**

Wondering what kind of animal is causing trouble in your yard? See if you can spot its tracks.

# NATURE'S BALANCE

It can be hard to think about shooting a cute little animal. However, good hunters don't want to make animals suffer. In your hunting safety class, you will learn how to make a clean kill. This puts the animal down quickly so it feels the least amount of pain.

Hunters love the outdoors and care about nature. Money from hunting licenses and other taxes helps pay for **conservation** efforts. This money keeps land clean and animal populations healthy for all nature lovers to enjoy.

RED FOX

Hunting laws are in place to keep people and animals safe.

# GLOSSARY

**breed:** a group of animals that share features different from other groups of the kind

**challenge:** a test of abilities

**compound:** made up of two or more parts

**conservation:** the care of the natural world

**habitat:** the place or type of place where an animal naturally or normally lives or grows

**license:** a piece of paper that allows someone to do something

**mammal:** a warm-blooded animal that has a backbone and hair, breathes air, and feeds milk to its young

**pulley:** a wheel or combination of wheels used with a rope to move heavy objects

**related:** connected by family

**target:** the focus of effort

**traditional:** having to do with long-practiced customs

**weapon:** something used to cause someone or something injury or death

# FOR MORE INFORMATION

## BOOKS

Gurtler, Janet. *Small Game*. New York, NY: AV2 Books, 2017.

Uhl, Xina M. *Insider Tips for Hunting Small Game*. New York, NY: Rosen Central, 2018.

## WEBSITES

**Hunting Dog Facts for Kids**
*kids.kiddle.co/Hunting_dog*
Learn about types of hunting dogs and see pictures of different breeds.

**Hunter-Ed**
*hunter-ed.com*
View study guides and take state-approved hunting safety courses online.

# INDEX

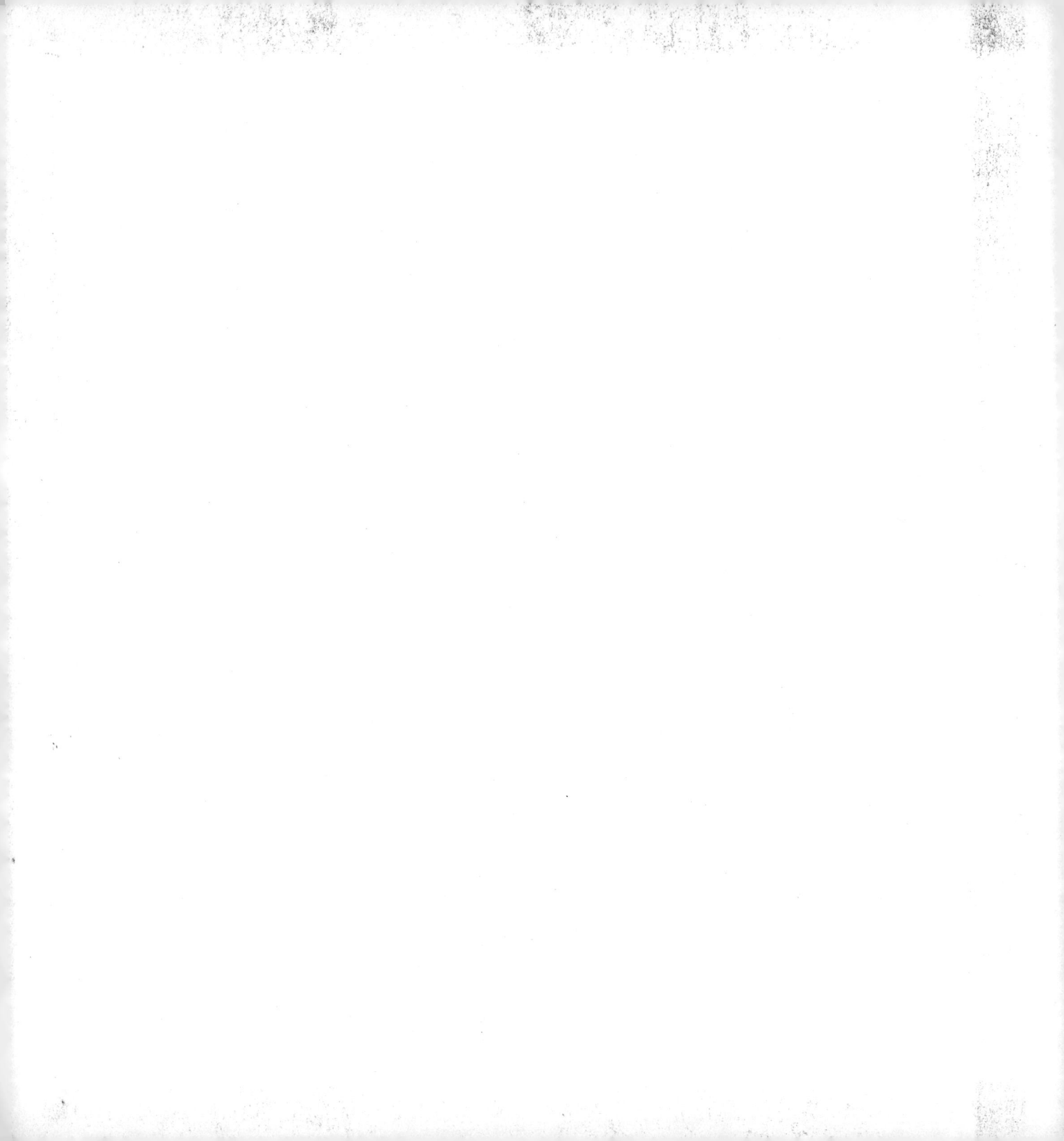